Dreamland

A Lullaby by Mary Chapin Carpenter

Pictures by Julia Noonan

HarperCollinsPublishers

This book is dedicated with love and sweet dreams to

Christopher, Alexander, Madeline, Bobby, Katie, Hannah,

Stephen, Leslie, Annie, Chapin, and Carter

from their aunt Mary Chapin.

—M.C.C.

For my own exceptional Anna Claire

and in memory of Grandma Clara

—J.N.

Special thanks to Sonia.

Art was prepared with oil on paper.

Text copyright © 1996 by Mary Chapin Carpenter and EMI April Music Inc.
Pictures copyright © 1996 by Julia Noonan
All rights reserved. No part of this book may be used or reproduced in any manner whatso-
ever without written permission except in the case of brief quotations embodied in critical
articles and reviews. Printed in the United States of America. For information address
HarperCollins Children's Books, a division of HarperCollins Publishers,
10 East 53rd Street, New York, NY 10022.

Library of Congress Cataloging-in-Publication Data
Carpenter, Mary Chapin.
  Dreamland, a lullaby by Mary Chapin Carpenter/ pictures by Julia Noonan.
    p.   cm.
  Summary: As the stars whisper a lullaby at bedtime, the man in the moon and the Milky
Way welcome a child to dreamland.
  ISBN 0-06-025402-5. — ISBN 0-06-025403-3 (lib. bdg.)
  [1. Bedtime-Fiction. 2. Lullabies. 3. Stories in rhyme.] I. Noonan, Julia, ill. II. Title.
PZ8.3.C1995Dr   1996   95-16576
[E]—dc20   CIP
                                                                             AC

1 2 3 4 5 6 7 8 9 10
❖
First Edition

DREAMLAND was originally a song, inspired and written as part of a CD of music to benefit the Voiceless Victims project of the Institute For Intercultural Understanding. Available from Columbia Records, the CD is entitled "'Til Their Eyes Shine: The Lullaby Album." An accompanying video of the participating artists performing their songs is called "Child of Mine: The Lullaby Video" and is also available from Columbia Home Video. Proceeds from the CD, video, and this book will be donated to the Institute to further their work in providing multicultural education, assistance, and support to children and adults around the world. I wish to gratefully acknowledge Rosanne Cash, who initiated and coordinated each artist's involvement with this benefit project, and the Institute For Intercultural Understanding for their continuing efforts to improve the lives of children around the world.   —M.C.C.

If you would like to learn more about the Voiceless Victims project, please contact the Institute For Intercultural Understanding at:
2025 Maryland Avenue · Louisville, KY 40205 · (502) 454-0607

'Til Their Eyes Shine: The Lullaby Album available on Columbia Records, Catalog #52412
Child of Mine: The Lullaby Video available on Columbia Home Video, Catalog #49155

Sun goes down
and says good night,

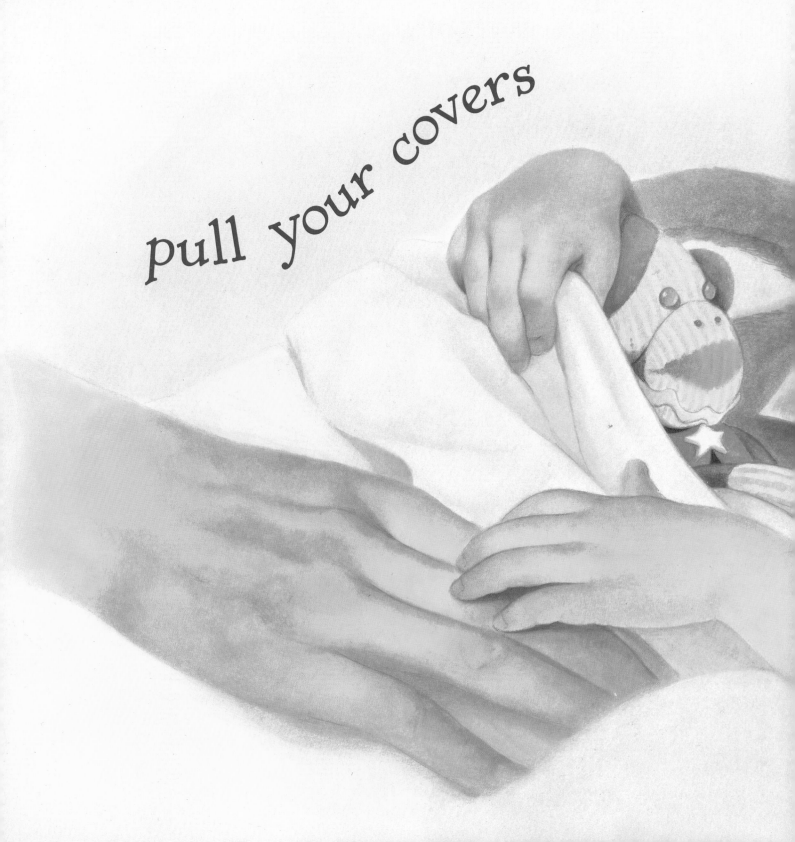

pull your covers

up real tight.

By your bed we'll leave a light

to guide you off to

dreamland.

Your pillow's soft,

your bed is warm.

Your eyes are tired

when day is done.

One more kiss

and you'll be gone,

on your way

to dreamland.

Every sleepy boy and girl, in

every bed around the world,

can hear the stars
up in the sky

whispering a lullaby.

winging past the
light of day?

The man in the moon and the Milky Way welcome you

to dreamland.

Every sleepy
boy and girl,

in every bed around the world,

can hear the stars
up in the sky

whispering

a lullaby.

Who knows where
you'll fly away,

winging past the
light of day?

The man in the moon and the Milky Way

welcome you to dreamland.